Henry Tennyson Folkard

A Lindsay Record

being a handlist of books written by or relating to members of the clan

Lindsay

Henry Tennyson Folkard

A Lindsay Record
being a handlist of books written by or relating to members of the clan Lindsay

ISBN/EAN: 9783337389932

Printed in Europe, USA, Canada, Australia, Japan

Cover: Foto ©Andreas Hilbeck / pixelio.de

More available books at **www.hansebooks.com**

DEDICATED

To the Right Hon. the Earl of Crawford,

K.T., LL.D., F.R.S., ETC.,

The Head of the Clan Lindsay,

AND

Chairman of the Committee

OF THE

Wigan Free Public Library.

Copyright

HAIGH HALL LIBRARY.

A. Rudolph-Douglas, Wigan

A LINDSAY RECORD: BEING A HAND-LIST OF BOOKS WRITTEN BY OR RELATING TO MEMBERS OF THE CLAN LINDSAY: PRESERVED IN THE REFERENCE DEPARTMENT OF THE WIGAN FREE PUBLIC LIBRARY. BY HENRY TENNYSON FOLKARD, F.S.A.

Lindsay Family. History and Traditions of the Land of the Lindsays, etc., by Andrew Jervise. 2nd edition. [*Plates*]. 8vo. Edinb. 1882.

Lindsay Family. Lives of the Lindsays, by Alexander William, Earl of Crawford and Balcarres. 4 vols. 4to. Wigan, 1840.

Lindsay Family. The Lindsays in India, by Sir John W. Kaye.—*Selections from the Calcutta Review.* *vol.* 4. 1882.

Lindsay Family. The Lindsays in Lancashire, by W. E. A. Axon. [*Lancashire Gleanings.*] sm. 4to. Manch. 1883.

Lindsay Family. The Lindsays of America, by Margaret I. Lindsay. sm. 4to. Albany, N.Y., 1889.

Lindsay (Alexander, *fourth Earl of Crawford, "Earl Beardie"*; *d.* 1454.) [Life of Alexander Lindsay, fourth Earl of Crawford, by T. F. Henderson.]— *Stephen (L.) and Lee (S.) Dictionary of National Biography. vol.* 33. 1893.

Lindsay (Alexander, *bishop of Dunkeld*, 1570?-1639.)
[Life of Alexander Lindsay, bishop of Dunkeld,
by T. F. Henderson.]—*Stephen (L.) and Lee (S.)
Dictionary of National Biography. vol.* 33. 1893.

Lindsay (Alexander, *first Lord Spynie*, 1560?-1607.)
[Life of Alexander Lindsay, first Lord Spynie,
by T. F. Henderson.]—*Stephen (L.) and Lee (S.)
Dictionary of National Biography. vol.* 33. 1893.

Lindsay (Alexander, *second Lord Spynie*, 1590?-1646.)
[Life of Alexander Lindsay, second Lord Spynie,
by T. F. Henderson.]—*Stephen (L.) and Lee (S.)
Dictionary of National Biography. vol.* 33. 1893.

Lindsay (Alexander, *second Lord Balcarres and first
Earl of Balcarres*, 1618-1659.) An account of any
accession the Earl of Balcarres had to the late
engagement; with a justification of the letter
written by his Lordship to the Committee of
Estates, 1649. — Letter from the Right Hon.
Alexander, Earl of Balcarres, to His Majesty
King Charles II. 1654.—*Maidment (J.) Historical
Fragments, etc.*, 1833.

60 copies only, printed.

— [Life of Alexander Lindsay, first Earl of Balcarres,
by T. F. Henderson.]—*Stephen (L.) and Lee (S.)
Dictionary of National Biography. vol.* 33. 1893.

Lindsay (Alexander, *sixth Earl of Balcarres*, 1752-1825.)
Extracts from Official Correspondence.—*Lindsay
(A. W. C.) Lives of the Lindsays, etc. vol.* 3. 1840.

— [Life of Alexander Lindsay, sixth Earl of Balcarres,
by T. F. Henderson.]—*Stephen (L.) and Lee (S.)
Dictionary of National Biography. vol.* 33. 1893.

Lindsay (*Sir* Alexander, *general*, 1785-1872.) [Life of
Sir Alexander Lindsay, by H. Manners Chichester.]
—*Stephen (L.) and Lee (S.) Dictionary of National
Biography. vol.* 33. 1893.

Lindsay (Alexander William Crawford, *twenty-fifth Earl
of Crawford and eighth Earl of Balcarres, Baron
Wigan*, 1812-1880.) Argo : or, the Quest of the
Golden Fleece. A metrical tale in ten books.
8vo. Lond. 1876.

— Ballads, Songs, and Poems, translated from
the German. *Privately printed.* 4to. Wigan, 1841.

Large paper copy.

— Brief analysis of the doctrine and argument in
the case of Gorham *v.* the Bishop of Exeter ; and
observations on the present position of the Church
of England with reference to the recent decision.
8vo. Lond. 1850.

— Considerations on the present question of the
Corn-Laws, submitted to the thinking minds of
England. [4 *pp., signed Lælius.*] sm. 4to. n.p.
[1846 ?]

Lindsay (Alexander William Crawford, *twenty-fifth Earl of Crawford, etc.*)—*continued*.

— The Creed of Japhet, that is of the race popularly surnamed Indo-Germanic or Aryan, as held before the period of its dispersion; ascertained by the aid of comparative mythology and language. [*One hundred and fifty copies printed for private circulation, copy* 30.] 8vo. Lond. 1891.

> With a preface by Margaret Lindsay, Countess of Crawford and Balcarres.

— The Earldom of Mar in sunshine and in shade during five hundred years. With incidental notices of the leading cases of Scottish dignities, from the reign of King Charles I. till now. In reply to an address to the Peers of Scotland, by Walter Henry, Earl of Kellie, May, 1879. Letters to the Lord Clerk Register of Scotland (George Frederick, Earl of Glasgow, Lord Boyle, etc.) 2 vols. 8vo. Edinb. 1882.

> Edited by Margaret Lindsay, Countess of Crawford and Balcarres.

— Etruscan Inscriptions analysed, translated, and commented upon. 8vo. Lond. 1872.

— Idas; or, Antichristus Britannicus, inter pocula. An extravaganza, by Johannes Boustrophedonides, solutus aratro. *Privately printed*. sm. 4to. Edinb. 1875.

Lindsay (Alexander William Crawford, *twenty-fifth Earl of Crawford, etc.*)—*continued.*

— A Letter to a Friend [*Sir Robert Holt Leigh*], on the Evidences and Theory of Christianity. 12mo. Lond. 1841.

— Letters on Egypt, Edom, and the Holy Land. 2nd. edition. [*Frontispieces.*] 2 vols. 4to. Lond. 1838.

Large paper copy.

— [The same.] Third edition. [*Frontispieces.*] 2 vols. 12mo. Lond. 1839.

— [The same.] Fourth edition, revised and corrected. [*Frontispiece.*] sm. 8vo. Lond. 1847.

— Lives of the Lindsays; or, a Memoir of the Houses of Crawford and Balcarres, etc. To which are added extracts from the official correspondence of Alexander, sixth Earl of Balcarres, during the Maroon War; together with personal narratives by his brothers, the Hon. Robert, Colin, James, John, and Hugh Lindsay. 4 vols. 4to. Wigan, 1840.

Privately printed copy on largest paper.

— [Another copy.] 4 vols. roy. 8vo. Wigan, 1840.

Presentation copy to the Rev. John Hamilton Gray; containing his bookplate, and a letter from the author inserted.

— [Another edition.] 3 vols. 8vo. Lond. 1849.

Lindsay (Alexander William Crawford, *twenty-fifth Earl of Crawford, etc.*)—*continued.*

— A Memoir of Lady Anna Mackenzie, Countess of Balcarres, and afterwards of Argyll, 1621-1706. [*Portrait.*] sm. 8vo. Edinb. 1868.

— Mémoires d'une Poupée. Autobiographical memoirs of the life and adventures of a Doll. Freely translated from the French of Mlle. Louise D'Aulnoy [*by the Earl of Crawford and Balcarres.*] sm. 8vo. Lond. 1840.

— Œcumenicity in relation to the Church of England. Four letters : i. On the Catholicity of the Anglican Church : ii. On the claims of England *versus* Rome : iii. On the futility of attempts at Renconciliation with the Church of Rome : iv. On the (so called) Œcumenical Council of 1869-70. With an appendix on the Ultramontane and Gallican theories in relation to Œcumenicity and the Church of England. 8vo. Lond. 1870.

— On the theory of the English Hexameter, and its applicability to the translation of Homer. 8vo. Lond. 1862.

— Poems and Poetical Fragments. 4to. Wigan, 1838.

Large paper copy.

— [Another copy.] sm. 8vo. Wigan, 1838.

On the fly leaf is written : " Mrs. Dawson Pennant with the Author's brother's kind regards, 1845."

Lindsay (Alexander William Crawford, *twenty-fifth Earl of Crawford, etc.*)—*continued*.

— [Another copy.] sm. 8vo. Wigan, 1838.

— Progression by Antagonism : a theory, involving considerations touching the present position, duties, and destiny of Great Britain. 8vo. Lond. 1846.

— Report of the Speeches of Counsel (Sir F. Kelly, Sir R. Bethell, Sir A. J. E. Cockburn, the Lord Advocate) and of the Lord Chancellor [R. M. Rolfe, Baron Cranworth and Lord St. Leonard's in moving the resolution, upon the claim of James, Earl of Crawford, etc., to the original Dukedom of Montrose. fol. Lond. 1856.

— [Review of " The Book of Carlaverock."] 8vo. Lond. 1874.

— Scepticism a retrogressive movement in theology and philosophy, as contrasted with the Church of England, Catholic (at once) and Protestant, stable and progressive : two letters on points of present interest, addressed to W. B. Bryan, rector of Rodington, etc., and the Hon. Colin Lindsay. 8vo. Lond. 1861.

> Presentation copy to the Rev. John Hamilton Gray ; containing his bookplate, and two letters from the author inserted.

— [Another copy.] 8vo. Lond. 1874.

Lindsay (Alexander William Crawford, *twenty-fifth Earl Crawford, etc.*)—*continued*.

— Sertum Horatianum : twelve odes. Selected and translated by Linus. 8vo. Lond. 1874.

— Sketches of the History of Christian Art. 3 vols. 8vo. Lond. 1874.

— [The same.] 2nd edition. 2 vols. 8vo. Lond. [*Edinb. printed.*] 1885.

> With a "Notice" by Margaret Lindsay, Countess of Crawford and Balcarres.

— [Lord Lindsay's History of Christian Art, by John Ruskin.]—*Quarterly Review, vol.* 81. 1847.

— Two Letters :—To an Italian priest, on the Catholicity of the Church of England ; and to an English clergyman, on the futility of attempts at Reconciliation with the Church of Rome. 8vo. Lond. 1866.

— The True Story of Lord and Lady Byron, as told by Lord Macaulay, Thomas Moore, Leigh Hunt, . Thomas Campbell, the Countess of Blessington, Lord Lindsay, etc. sm. 8vo. Lond. [1869.]

— [The Dun Echt Outrage. A collection of newspaper cuttings, relating to the stealing of the body of the Earl of Crawford and Balcarres.] 4to. Aberdeen, London, Wigan, etc., 1882-86.

Lindsay (Alexander William Crawford, *twenty-fifth Earl of Crawford, etc.*)—*continued.*

— [Life of Alexander William Crawford Lindsay, twenty-fifth Earl of Crawford, etc., by W. A. J. Archbold.]—*Stephen (L.) and Lee (S.) Dictionary of National Biography. vol.* 33. 1893.

Lindsay, afterwards Barnard (Lady Anne, *authoress of the ballad of 'Auld Robin Gray,'* 1750-1825.) Auld Robin Gray [*with the Continuations; and Versions from the German by Lady Margaret Lindsay.*] *Privately printed.* roy. 8vo. Wigan, 1840.

— [Life of Lady Anne Barnard, by A. Vere Benson.] —*Stephen (L.) and Lee (S.) Dictionary of National Biography. vol.* 3. 1885.

Lindsay (Beatrice, c. s., *of Girton College, Cambridge.*) An introduction to the study of Zoology. With one hundred and twenty-four illustrations and diagrams. 8vo. Lond. 1899.

Lindsay (*Lady* Caroline Blanche Elizabeth). About Robins. Songs, facts, and legends, collected and illustrated by Lady Lindsay. [With a facsimile of one of Thomas Morley's " Canzonets to three voyces."] 4to. Lond. [1889.]

— The Apostle of the Ardennes. sm. 8vo. Lond. 1899.

Lindsay (*Lady* Caroline Blanche Elizabeth)—*continued.*

— The Art of Poetry with regard to Women writers. A paper read at the Literature Meeting of the Women's International Congress, St. Martin's Great Hall, on Wednesday, June 28th, 1899. sm. 8vo. [Lond. 1899.]

— The Flower Seller, and other poems. sm. 8vo. Lond. 1896.

— The King's last Vigil, and other poems. sm. 8vo. Lond. 1894.

— Miss Dairsie's Diary; A fragment. [*Extracted from Temple Bar.*] 8vo. Lond. 1883.

— Passages from the Diary of an Artist. 8vo. Lond. [1875.]

— Waldemar's Violin, a tale. [*Extracted from Warne's Illustrated Annual.*] 8vo. Lond. 1880.

Lindsay (Colin, *third Earl of Balcarres*, 1654 ?-1722.) An account of the affairs of Scotland, relating to the Revolution of 1688, as sent to the late King James II. when in France, never before printed, etc. [*With a Key to the Account, etc.*] sm. 8vo. Lond. 1714.

Lindsay (Colin, *third Earl of Balcarres*)—*continued*.

— [Another edition.]—*Somers' Tracts, vol.* 11. *p.* 487.

— Memoirs touching the Revolution in Scotland, 1688 - 1690. Presented to King James II. at St. Germains, 1690. Printed for the Bannatyne Club. 4to. Edinb. 1841.

— [Life of Colin Lindsay, third Earl of Balcarres, by T. F. Henderson.]—*Stephen (L.) and Lee (S.) Dictionary of National Biography. vol.* 33. 1893.

Lindsay (*Hon.* Colin, *lieut.-colonel,* 1755-1795.) Extracts from Colonel Tempelhoffe's History of the Seven Years' War: his remarks on General Lloyd: on the subsistence of armies; and on the march of convoys. Also a treatise on winter posts: To which is added a narrative of events at St. Lucie and Gibraltar, and of John Duke of Marlborough's march to the Danube, etc. [*Plans.*]. 2 vols. 8vo. Lond. 1793.

— Narrative of the occupation and defence of St. Lucie, 1779; and of the Siege of Gibraltar, 1782. —*Lindsay (A. W. C.) Lives of the Lindsays, etc. vol.* 3. 1840. ·

— [Another edition.]—*Oriental Miscellanies, etc.* 1840.

Lindsay (*Hon.* Colin, *son of James, twenty-fourth Earl of Crawford, etc.*, 1819-1892.) The Anglican Altar. An Address to the Members and Associates of the English Church Union, on the opening of the Session for 1866-7. sm. 8vo. Lond. 1867.

— The Choir of the Parish Church [*of Wigan.*] sm. 8vo. Wigan, 1853.—*Wigan Local Pamphlets, vol. 7.*

— De Ecclesia et Cathedra; or, the Empire-Church of Jesus Christ. 2 vols. 8vo. Lond. 1877.

— Defence of the orthodox party in the Church of England. A letter to his grace the Duke of Manchester, in reply to a circular issued by his grace as president of the National Club, which has been circulated among the churchwardens and magistrates of England. 8vo. Lond. 1851.

— The Evidence for the Papacy as derived from the Holy Scriptures and from primitive antiquity. With an introductary epistle. 8vo. Lond. 1870.

> " To the memory of One lately deceased, who when in life expressed a desire that the author of this work would state in writing the grounds which led to his conversion to the Catholic Church. Requiescat in pace. ✚ "

— The Feast of Easter [*and*] the Church of England. 8vo. Wigan, 1849.

Lindsay (*Hon.* Colin)—*continued.*

— Increase of the Episcopate and right of free election. A Petition to the House of Lords: with notes and observations, etc., by the Hon. Colin Lindsay. sm. 8vo. Lond. 1863.

— Mary, Queen of Scots, and her marriage with Bothwell. Seven letters to the "Tablet." sm. 8vo. Lond. 1883.

— Organisation, and the duties of members and associates. An address to the members and associates of the English Church Union. sm. 8vo. Lond. 1861.

— The Ornaments of the Church not Catholic only but Scriptural: a lecture delivered at Brighton and Liverpool. Published by request. sm. 8vo. Lond. 1866.

— Present position of Assistant or Stipendiary Curates. 8vo. Lond. [1866.]

— Report of the Council of the English Church Union relative to the preparation of the Memorials on Ritual, and of their presentation to the Archbishop of Canterbury, etc., on Saturday, 3rd February, 1866. 8vo. Lond. 1866.

— Report submitted to the Manchester Church Society, by a Committee appointed for that purpose, on the Nomination and Election of Bishops. 8vo. Oxford, [*Manchester printed.*] 1860.

Lindsay (*Hon.* Colin)—*continued.*

— Report submitted to the Manchester Church Society, by a Committee appointed for that purpose, on the Royal Supremacy and Church Emancipation, etc. 8vo. Oxford, 1857.

— Reply [*to Lord John Russell on Dr. Hampden's appointment to the See of Hereford.*] 12mo. n.d.

— Right of all the Parishoners to the free use of their Parish Church, etc. An address delivered at Manchester, before the Society for promoting the Restoration of Churches to the People, etc. 8vo. Manch. 1859.

— Sisters of Mercy. [*Letter to the Editor of the Wigan Times.*] 8vo. Wigan, 1850.

— Tradition, Easter, and the Church. A reply to "The Protestant Layman." 8vo. Wigan, 1849.

— Two Letters addressed to the Editor of the Wigan Examiner. i. The Sanctity of Sunday as the Lord's Sabbath. ii. Consideration of a plan for giving the Working Classes a Holiday once a month ; without loss either to master or men. 12mo. Wigan, 1856.

Lindsay (*Sir* Coutts, BART.) Alfred, a drama [*in three acts and in verse*]. 8vo. Lond. 1845.

— Boadicea, a tragedy [*in three acts and in verse*]. 8vo. Lond. 1857.

Lindsay (*Sir* Coutts, BART)—*continued.*

— Edward the Black Prince. A tragedy [*in three acts and in verse*]. sm. 8vo. Lond. 1846.

Lindsay (*Sir* David, *first Earl of Crawford*, 1365?-1407.) [Life of Sir David Lindsay, first Earl of Crawford, by T. F. Henderson.]—*Stephen* (*L.*) *and Lee* (*S.*) *Dictionary of National Biography. vol.* 33. 1893.

Lindsay (David, *fifth Earl of Crawford and first Duke of Montrose*, 1440?-1495.) [Life of David Lindsay, fifth Earl of Crawford, etc., by T. F. Henderson.] *Stephen* (*L.*) *and Lee* (*S.*) *Dictionary of National Biography. vol.* 33. 1893.

Lindsay or Lyndsay (*Sir* David, *Scottish poet and Lyon King of Arms*, 1490-1555.) Works of the famous and worthy knight, Sir David Lindesay of the Mount, *alias* Lyon King at Armes. Newly corrected, etc. [*Black letter.*] sm. 8vo. Edinb. 1670.

— Sir David Lindsay's Works. [*Edited by F. Hall, J. Small, J. A. H. Murray, etc.*] *Early English Text Society* (*vols.* 11, 19, 35, 37, 47.) 8vo. Lond. 1865-71.

— The Poetical Works of Sir David Lyndsay, of the Mount, etc. A new edition carefully revised [*by David Laing.*] 2 vols. sm. 8vo. Edinb. 1871.

Lindsay (*Sir* David)—*continued.*

— The Complaynt of Scotland, etc. 1549. [*Attributed to Sir David Lyndsay.*] Re-edited from the originals, with introduction and glossary, by J. A. H. Murray. *Early English Text Society, extra series* (*vol.* 17.) 8vo. Lond. 1872.

— [Life of Sir David Lindsay, by A. Mackay.]— *Stephen* (*L.*) *and Lee* (*S.*) *Dictionary of National Biography. vol.* 33. 1893.

Lindsay (David, *eleventh Earl of Crawford*, 1547?-1607.) [Life of David Lindsay, eleventh Earl of Crawford, by T. F. Henderson.]—*Stephen* (*L.*) *and Lee* (*S.*) *Dictionary of National Biography. vol.* 33. 1893.

Lindsay (David, *twelfth Earl of Crawford*, 1565?-1621.) [Life of David Lindsay, twelfth Earl of Crawford, by T. F. Henderson.]—*Stephen* (*L.*) *and Lee* (*S.*) *Dictionary of National Biography. vol.* 33. 1893.

Lindsay (*Sir* David, *of Edzell*, 1551?-1610.) [Life of Sir David Lindsay of Edzell, by T. F. Henderson.] *Stephen* (*L.*) *and Lee* (*S.*) *Dictionary of National Biography. vol.* 33. 1893.

Lindsay (David, *bishop of Ross*, 1531?-1613.) [Life of David Lindsay, Bishop of Ross, by T. F. Henderson.]—*Stephen* (*L.*) *and Lee* (*S.*) *Dictionary of National Biography. vol.* 33. 1893.

Lindsay (David, *presbyterian divine*, 1566?-1627.) The Godly Man's journey to Heaven; containing ten several treatises, etc. sm. 8vo. Lond. 1625.

— [Life of David Lindsay, by T. F. Henderson.]— *Stephen (L.) and Lee (S.) Dictionary of National Biography. vol.* 33. 1893.

Lindsay (David, *bishop of Edinburgh; d.* 1641.) [Life of David Lindsay, Bishop of Edinburgh, by F. Hindes Groome.]—*Stephen (L.) and Lee (S.) Dictionary of National Biography. vol.* 33. 1893.

Lindsay (David, *secretary to the Earl of Melfort.*) Trial of David Lindsay, at the Old Bailey for High Treason, 1704.—*Howell (T. B.) State Trials, etc. vol.* 14. 1816.

Lindsay (*Hon.* Edwin Hugh, *b.* 1786.) Earl Balcarres and the Hon. Edwin Hugh Lindsay, a narrative of authentic facts, etc., 1837.—*Lindsay (James, 24th Earl of Crawford, etc.*)

Lindsay (George, *third Lord Spynie,* 1600?-1671.) [Life of George Lindsay, third Lord Spynie, by T. F. Henderson.]—*Stephen (L.) and Lee (S.) Dictionary of National Biography. vol.* 33. 1893.

Lindsay (*Hon.* Hugh, *director of the East India Company,* 1765?-1844.) An Adventure in China.—*Lindsay (A. W. C.) Lives of the Lindsays, etc. vol.* 4. 1840.

— [Another edition.] *Oriental Miscellanies, etc.* 1840.

Lindsay (*Sir* James, *ninth Lord Crawford; d.* 1396.) [Life of Sir James Lindsay, ninth Lord of Crawford, by T. F. Henderson.]—*Stephen (L.) and Lee (S.) Dictionary of National Biography. vol.* 33. 1893.

— [Sir James Lindsay of Crawford.]—*Burke (Sir J. B.) Anecdotes of the Aristocracy, etc. second series, vol.* 2. 1850.

Lindsay (James, *twenty-fourth Earl of Crawford and seventh Earl of Balcarres, Baron Wigan,* 1783-1869.) Case of James, Earl of Balcarres, etc., claiming the titles, honours and dignities of the Earldom of Crawford, and older Barony of Lindsay. fol. Lond. [1845 ?]

— Case of James, Earl of Crawford and Balcarres, etc., claiming the title, honour, and dignity of the original Dukedom of Montrose, created in 1488. fol. Lond. [1850 ?]

— Abstract of the Case of James, Earl of Crawford and Balcarres, claiming the original Dukedom of Montrose, created in 1488. Lond. 1850.—Abstract of the Supplemental Case, etc. Lond. 1852.— Abstract of the Case, etc., with reference to the petition and alleged right of James, Duke of Montrose to be admitted as a party in opposition to the said claim. Lond. 1851.—Analysis of the objections started by the Crown, and of the

Lindsay (James, *twenty-fourth Earl of Crawford, etc.*)—*continued.*

replies furnished by J. Riddell, etc. Lond. 1847.— Analysis of the Case for James, Duke of Montrose, petitioner, etc. [*Five pamphlets, bound together, the first four written by John Riddell.*]8vo. Lond. 1847-52.

— Earl Balcarres and the Hon. Edwin Hugh Lindsay, a narrative of authentic facts connected with the detention of the Brother of the noble Earl of Balcarres on the Island of Papa Stour, South Shetland, for a period of twenty-six years, and his providential escape from thence through the agency of the Society of Friends : the original letters of the noble Earl, and the reply of the persecuted Brother. To which is subjoined a short account of Miss Watson and Captain Pilkington, together with a brief description of the Shetland Isles, etc., by Ebenezer. 8vo. Lond. 1837.

— Report of the Speeches of Counsel, etc., upon the Claim of James Earl of Crawford, etc., to the original Dukedom of Montrose, 1855.—*Lindsay (A. W. C.)*

Lindsay (*Sir* James, *general;* M.P. *for Wigan,* 1845-57, *and* 1859-66; 1815-74.) Narrative of the Red River Expedition, by an Officer of the Expeditionary Force. [*Extracted from Blackwood's Magazine,* 1870-71.] 8vo. Edinb. 1871.

Lindsay (*Sir* James)—*continued.*

— The Royal Warrant of the 6th October, 1854, and its effect on the Lieut.-Colonels in the army who had obtained that rank before the 20th of June, 1854. 8vo. Lond. 1857.—Memorandum upon the Memorial of the Brigade of Guards. 8vo. n.d.— Letter to the Officers of the Guards. 8vo. Lond. 1856.   Three pamphlets bound together.

Lindsay (*Hon.* James, *fourth son of James, fifth Earl of Balcarres.* 1758-1783.) Narrative of the Battle of Conjerveram, etc., 1780.—*Lindsay (A. W. C.) Lives of the Lindsays, etc. vol.* 4. 1840.

— [Another edition.]—*Oriental Miscellanies, etc.* 1840.

Lindsay (James, M.A., *minister of the parish of St. Andrew's, Kilmarnock.*) The Progressiveness of modern Christian thought. sm. 8vo. Edinb. 1892.

Lindsay (James Bowman, *weaver, schoolmaster and scholar,* 1799-1862.) The Chrono-Astrolabe ; containing a full set of Astronomic Tables, with rules and examples for the calculation of Eclipses and other celestial phenomena ; comprising also Plane and Spherical Trigonometry, and the most copious list of ancient eclipses ever published ; connected with these the dates of ancient events are exactly determined, and the authenticity of Hebrew,

Lindsay (James Bowman)—*continued*.

Greek, Roman, and Chinese writings is demon-
strated. 8vo. Dundee, 1858.

With a letter concerning the Author inserted, by
Alexander William, 25th Earl of Crawford, etc.

Lindsay (James Ludovic, *twenty-sixth Earl of Crawford
and ninth Earl of Balcarres, Baron Wigan*.) Address
delivered at the twenty-first Annual Meeting of
the Library Association, at Southport.—*Souvenir
of the 21st Annual Meeting at Southport, Preston,
Wigan*. 1898.

— Bibliorum Sacrorum exemplaria tam manuscripta,
quam impressa, quæ in Bibliotheca Lindesiana
adservantur. 8vo. Romæ, 1884.

Only 50 copies printed.

— Bibliotheca Lindesiana. Catalogue of a Collection
of English Ballads of the 17th and 18th Centuries;
printed for the most part in black-letter. sm. 4to.
[Aberdeen] 1890.

Only 100 copies privately printed.

— Bibliotheca Lindesiana. Catalogue of Chinese
Books and Manuscripts. sm. 4to. [Hertford] 1895.

Only 100 copies privately printed.

— Bibliotheca Lindesiana. Catalogue of English
Broadsides, 1505-1897. *Privately printed*. sm. 4to.
[Aberdeen.] 1898.

Only 100 copies printed,

Lindsay (James Ludovic, *twenty-sixth Earl of Crawford, etc.*)—*continued.*

— Bibliotheca Lindesiana. [Sale] Catalogue of the [first and second portions] Library of the Right Hon. the Earl of Crawford. [*Priced.*] 2 vols. imp. 8vo. Lond. 1887-89.

> No. i. of twenty-five copies printed on large paper. Containing introductions signed " Crawford."

— [Another copy.] 2 vols. roy. 8vo. Lond. 1887-89.

— Bibliotheca Lindesiana. Collations and Notes. No. 1. Sanderi Brabantia, 1656-1695. 4to. Lond. 1883.

— Bibliotheca Lindesiana. Collations and Notes. No. 2. Fowler's Mosaic Pavements, etc. 4to. Lond. 1883.

— Bibliotheca Lindesiana. Collations and Notes. No. 3. Grands et Petits Voyages of De Bry. 4to. Lond. 1884.

> " The copy now sent is on fine paper (five copies pulled) and it has autotype photographs in addition to the photolithographs. There is only one other copy thus treated, in H.M. Library at Windsor." Extract from a letter of Lord Crawford, inserted in the volume.

HAIGH HALL LIBRARY.

A. Rudolph-Douglas, Wigan

Lindsay (James Ludovic, *twenty-sixth Earl of Crawford, etc.*)—*continued.*

— Bibliotheca Lindesiana. Collation and Notes. No. 4. Autotype Facsimiles of three Mappemondes. i. Harleian (or anonymous) Mappemonde circa 1536. ii. Mappemonde by Desceliers of 1546. iii. The Mappemonde of Desceliers of 1550. With an introduction including a short notice on Desceliers' later Mappemonde of 1553, by C. H. Coote. *Privately printed.* 2 vols. fol. and 4to. Aberdeen, 1898.

One of 10 copies printed on fine paper.

— Bibliotheca Lindesiana. Hand list of the Boudoir Books. 8vo. Leipzig, 1881.

— Bibliotheca Lindesiana. Hand list of a Collection of Broadside Proclamations, issued by authority of the Kings and Queens of Great Britain and Ireland. 8vo. Lond. 1886.

— Bibliotheca Lindesiana. Hand-list of Proclamations. Tables of the Regnal years of the Sovereigns of England and Scotland. Henry VIII.—Victoria. sm. 4to. n.p. 1891.

— Bibliotheca Lindesiana. First Revision. Hand-list of Proclamations. Henry VIII.—William IV. 1509-1837. 2 vols. fol. Aberdeen, 1893-97.

Only 50 copies printed.

Lindsay (James Ludovic, *twenty-sixth Earl of Crawford, etc.)—continued.*

— Bibliotheca Lindesiana, Hand-list of Oriental Manuscripts. Arabic, Persian, Turkish. *Privately printed.* sm. 4to. [Aberdeen], 1898.

         Only 100 copies printed.

— Bibliotheca Lindesiana. Hand list of the early editions of the Greek and Latin Writers of ancient and mediæval times. To which are added a few of the rarer Vocabularies and Grammars of those languages. 8vo. Lond. 1885.

         Only 50 copies printed.

— Bibliotheca Lindesiana. List of Manuscripts and examples of Metal and Ivory Bindings, exhibited to the Bibliographical Society at the Grafton Galleries, 13th June, 1898, by the President. 8vo. Aberdeen, 1898.

— Bibliotheca Lindesiana. List of Manuscripts, Printed Books, and examples of Metal and Ivory Bindings, exhibited to the Library Association at Haigh Hall, 26th August, 1898, by the President. 8vo. Aberdeen, 1898.

— Bibliotheca Lindesiana. Upon the Facsimile Paintings and Publications of the Comte Auguste de Bastard D'Estang. 8vo. [Lond.] 1886.

Lindsay (James Ludovic, *twenty-sixth Earl of Crawford, etc.*)—*continued.*

— Dun Echt Observatory Publications. Advance sheets, subject to revision. Classification scheme, and Index to the same of the Library of the Observatory. 4to. Dun Echt, 1879.

— Dun Echt Observatory Publications. [vol. i.] A Summary or Index of the measurements in the "Stellarum duplicium et multiplicium mensuræ micrometricæ "—F. G. W. Struve, 1837; "Additamentum in F. G. W. Struve Mensuras micrometricas stellarum duplicium,"—editas anno 1837. Petrop., 1840. Including all the stars in the "Synopsis observationum de stellis duclicibus, in specula Dorpatensi, annis a 1814 ad 1824, per intrumenta minora perfectorum," P. 305 ; and in "II. Mensuræ micrometricæ," P. 315. Re-arranged in order of R. A., and the positions brought up to 1875. 4to. Dun Echt, Aberdeen [*London printed.*] 1876.

— Dun Echt Observatory Publications. [vols. ii.-iii.] Mauritius Expedition, 1874. [*Plates.*]. 2 vols. 4to. Dun Echt, Aberdeen [*London printed.*] 1877-85.

— Early Bindings, Broadsides, Proclamations and Ballads, exhibited by the Earl of Crawford, at the Soirée of the Society of Antiquaries, 23rd June, 1886. sm. 4to. [Lond. 1886.]

Lindsay (James Ludovic, *twenty-sixth Earl of Crawford, etc.*)—*continued.*

— [Index Rerum et Nominum.] 4to. Lond. [1886.]

" In giving me this Lord Crawford writes—' The Index rerum et nominum, to which there is no title-page, is merely a string of subjeéts or entries which will eventually form the index to the Contributions to the Ephemeral History of England. The Catalogue will consist of Traéts, or pamphlets, Proclamations, Broadsides, Political Squibs and Poems, and Ballads proper. The skeleton of the index is taken from ' Lemon's index,' but a vast number of other entries have to be entered into it. To facilitate the making of these entries I printed 10 Copies in /86, C.'—[*Signed.*] Brabourne, Jany. 10th, 1888, Haigh Hall." The above communication is written on the first blank page in the book.

— The Medal to Professor Asaph Hall, United States Navy, for his discovery and observations of the Satellites of Mars, and his determinations of their orbits. [Reprinted from the Monthly Notices of the Royal Astronomical Society.] 8vo. Lond. 1879.

— On some Early Manuscripts and Printed Books.— *Lancashire and Cheshire Antiquarian Society, Transactions. vol.* 1. 1884.

— [Original Manuscript [*from the Libri Collection*], arranged by the Right Hon. the Earl of Crawford to illustrate the Progress of Handwriting, and presented by his Lordship to the Wigan Free Public Library.] 2 vols. fol. v. d.

Lindsay (James Ludovic, *twenty-sixth Earl of Crawford, etc.*)—*continued.*

9th Century.

Carolingian :—Portion of a Treatise of St. Augustine.

10th Century.

Carolingian:—Portion of an Evangelistarium, written in Belgium or the Netherlands about A.D. 900 (2 leaves).

11th Century.

Two leaves of Priscian's Grammar.—A leaf (cut in two pieces) from a Lectionarium written in Germany early in the eleventh century.—Portion of the Codex Juris Civilis (French ? 2 leaves).—Portion of an Antiphonary (French or Flemish), first half of the eleventh century (2 leaves).—Portion of an Antiphonary, with Music; written in Germany or Holland in the eleventh century.—Fragment of a German Missal; eleventh century.—A leaf containing the Special Offices from a Missal or Breviary or Psalter, most probably the last; written (? in North Eastern France) in the second half of the eleventh century.— Portions of a Psalter with Music, probably German, of the second half of the eleventh century.—Three leaves of a Breviarium, written in Eastern France late in the eleventh century, with Music.—Two leaves of an Antiphonarium, written about the end of the eleventh century (? German).—Portion of a Lectionarium, written in Germany about the end of the eleventh century.

12th Century.

Portion of a Lectionarium, written probably in Germany about A.D. 1100.—Leaf from a Codex of the Latin Gospels of the twelfth century.—Part of an Antiphonarium about the beginning of the twelfth

Lindsay (James Ludovic, *twenty-sixth Earl of
Crawford, etc.)—continued.*

century.—Portion of a Calendar to a Missal; German,
twelfth century.—Portion of a Missal (Offertory),
German, twelfth century.—Portion of a Treatise by
a Schoolman, De Sanctis Ecclesia," written about
A.D. 1100 (2 leaves).—Part of a Homily, probably
beginning of the twelfth century; and three fragments
of the Old Testament (English, twelfth century).—
Part of an Antiphonarium, written probably in North
Italy in the first half of the twelfth century.—Portion
of the life of St. Nicholas of Myra, composed by John
the Deacon, afterwards Archdeacon of Bari, early in
the tenth century.—Two leaves of a Lectionarium,
apparently German (12th century).

13th Century.

Part of a Biblical MS. ; late thirteenth century ; and
part of a Breviary ; towards the end of the thirteenth
century.

14th Century.

Fragment of the Codex Juris Canonici (chiefly English
decisions), French MS. of about A.D. 1300.—Two
fragments of a Metrical Latin Grammar, about the
end of the thirteenth century.—Fragments from Ovid
(Amores ii., 5); French or English writing, end of
thirteenth or beginning of fourteenth century.—
Fragments of a Philosophical work ; probably in
an English handwriting, fourteenth century.—Two
Minatures: Birth and Crucifixion of Christ (? Italian),
thirteenth or fourteenth century ; and fragment of
MS. on Surgical science beginning of fourteenth
century.—Fragment of a Law Book, early fourteenth

Lindsay (James Ludovic, *twenty-sixth Earl of Crawford, etc.*)—*continued.*

century; and fragment of the Fabliau of Richaut, written in England early in the fourteenth century.—Part of Commentary on the "Hercules Œtæus" of Seneca, written about A.D. 1300-20 (English).—Fragment on the Law of Wills from the Codex Juris Civilis, beginning of the fourteenth century (French); and fragment of a work on Medicine and Diseases; probably English or French, beginning of fourteenth century.—Fragment of a set of Homilies, early fourteenth century.—Two leaves of an Antiphonarium (? Italian), curious for the antique character of the music as compared with the age of the writing.—Fragments of a Legal Treatise; of a Dutch or German Antiphonary; and of a French Church Service Book; all fourteenth century.—Part of the List of Hebrew names which is usually annexed to MS. of the Latin Bible (French).—Two fragments of an Antiphonarium (French, fourteenth century).—Two leaves of the Biblical History, translated into French by Guiart des Moulins, in 1291, from the Latin of Peter Comestor, French; first half of fourteenth century.—Portion of an Encyclopædic Dictionary (not the Catholicon); French handwriting, first half fourteenth century.—Portion of the "Roman de la Rose," written in French Flanders about 1350 (2 leaves).—Portion of a Missal; English, fourteenth century (2 leaves).—A Leaf of the Catholicon of Joannes de Balbis Januensis. Italian; fourteenth century.—Portion of the Rent Roll of a Monastery. English; fourteenth century (3 leaves).—Two Leaves

Lindsay (James Ludovic, *twenty-sixth Earl of Crawford, etc.*)—*continued.*

of an Antiphonarium, written in the second half of the fourteenth century.—Two Leaves of a Missal (Italian) of the fourteenth century.—Two Leaves of an Office of the Virgin (Minorite use). Italian handwriting; second half of fourteenth century.—Fragment of a Treatise on the Liturgical Division of the year, probably in an English hand; second half of fourteenth century.—Fragment of a Prayer Book; Italian hand, first half of fifteenth century.—Two Leaves or Fragments of a Martyrologium; Italian hand, close of fourteenth century.—Treatise on the Legal Prerogatives of the Church (relations of Church and State), English, fourteenth century (2 leaves).—Fragment of a Missal; Flemish or Dutch handwriting of fourteenth century; and Fragment of an Italian Choral book, fourteenth century.—Portion of Psalter (? English), fourteenth century.—Fragment of a Missal (perhaps English), late fourteenth century.—Lectionary, Dutch handwriting, beginning of fifteenth century: Prayer Book in Dutch, beginning of fifteenth century.

15th Century.

Portion of an Antiphonary (English), written A.D. 1400 (2 leaves).—Leaf of a Missal, probably written by a French hand, end of fourteenth or beginning of fifteenth century.—Portion of a Chronicle of Ancient History (? Miroir Historial), written about A.D. 1400 (2 leaves).—Leaf from a Treatise "de Dignitate Sacerdotali," about the beginning of the fifteenth

Lindsay (James Ludovic, *twenty-sixth Earl of Crawford, etc.)—continued.*

century; Italian hand.—Fragments of a Latin-French Glossary of Botanical words; probably written about the beginning of the fifteenth century.—Fragment of an English Poem of moral character on "The World" (? by Robert of Brunne), early fifteenth century.— Decisions of a Law Court in Marseilles in small cases; early part of fifteenth century. (The words constituting a libel in one case are given in the original Provençal (2 leaves).—Deed of Grant of Property, dated Grantham, 1440.—Fragment of an English Poem on "The World and the Flesh," early fifteenth century.—Rules of Health in connection with the seasons, in German, written about 1430; South Germany.—Treasury Note of Fines levied in cases tried at the Court held at Richmond in 1439.— Fragment of a Prayer-book containing a General Confession of Sins; in a High German dialect; Middle or first half of fifteenth century.—Portion of a Herbal (English), fifteenth century.—Assignment of Land in Gunwardeby (Gonerby in Lincolnshire), in 1464.—Fragment of a Psalter and Prayers, written in France about 1440-50.—Three Leaves from a Liber Officiorum or Breviary; in an Italian hand, middle of fifteenth century.

16th Century.

Bond for payment of money, about 1520.—Autograph of George Gascoigne, the dramatic poet; in his early days (about 1555), on the margin of a fifteenth-century treatise on the Exorcism of Demons.— Thomas Kyd's Account of Outlays for Clothing,

Lindsay (James Ludovic, *twenty-sixth Earl of Crawford, etc.*)—*continued*.

> dated 1557 (English).—Record of Grant (under Maximilian II.), 1567, concerning Monasteries, etc., in the District of Liége (2 leaves).—Memoranda of Births (Fisher family), 1586-89.—List of English landed properties, about 1590-1600 (2 leaves).—Rent-roll of Hather, Asby, Calverthorp, about 1590-1600.

> 18th Century.
> List of Middlesex Jurors, with autograph signature of Lord Mansfield, about 1760.

— [Original Collection of Papal Bulls, Edicts, Banns, etc., from 1538 to 1692. Presented to the Wigan Free Public Library by the Right Hon. the Earl of Crawford.] 3 vols. fol. & 4to. v.d.

— [Original Specimens of Oriental Penmanship, arranged by the Right Hon. the Earl of Crawford, and presented by his Lordship to the Wigan Free Public Library]. 6 vols. fol. v.d.

— [Photographs of Bindings, historic and artistic, belonging to the Right Hon. the Earl of Crawford.] fol. 1894.

— Screw-Cutting Tables, for Engineers and Machinists, giving the values of the different trains of wheels required to produce screws of any pitch. ob. 4to. Lond. 1878.

Lindsay (James Ludovic, *twenty-sixth Earl of Crawford, etc.*)—*continued.*

— Second International Library Conference. List of Manuscripts, Printed Books, and examples of Binding, exhibited to the American Librarians on the occasion of their visit to Haigh Hall. sm. 8vo. Aberdeen, 1897.

— Tables for ascertaining the Factor for a Billiard Player. Based on Major-General Drayson's suggestions in his work, "Billiards," pp. 76-84. Calculated by the Earl of Crawford, F.R.S., etc. 8vo. Wigan, 1890.

> Only 50 copies printed.

— [Tracts from the Lindsay Library. A volume with no title-page so lettered.] fol. n.d.

> " The catalogue called " *Tracts* " is a list of those which are bound together in 552 vols. and kept in the Library at Haigh. For convenience I catalogued them (some ten or twelve years ago) *as they were bound;* I printed 10 copies; I have cut up one of the copies and arranged them in order of date, as I think that to be perhaps the most useful way for using them. The Tracts themselves I intend to rebind separately, then I shall add the slips of a great number of others that I have, and reprint the whole as forming a class of the Contributions to the Ephemeral History of England. C."—" The above was written by Lord Crawford at Haigh Hall on 9th January, 1888, when he gave me this one of the ten copies referred to above. [*Signed*] Brabourne, March 12th, 1888."

Lindsay (John, *bishop of Glasgow; d.* 1335.) [Life of John Lindsay, Bishop of Glasgow, by A. H. Millar.]—*Stephen (L.) and Lee (S.) Dictionary of National Biography. vol.* 33. 1893.

Lindsay (John, *fifth Lord Lindsay of the Byres; d.* 1563.) [Life of John, fifth Lord Lindsay of the Byres, by T. F. Henderson.]—*Stephen (L.) and Lee (S.) Dictionary of National Biography. vol.* 33. 1893.

Lindsay (John, *Lord Menmuir, secretary of state in Scotland,* 1552-1598.) [Life of John Lindsay, Lord Menmuir, by T. F. Henderson.]—*Stephen (L.) and Lee (S.) Dictionary of National Biography. vol.* 33. 1893.

Lindsay (John, *tenth Lord Lindsay of the Byres, first Earl of Lindsay, and afterwards known as John Crawford-Lindsay, seventeenth Earl of Crawford,* 1596-1678.) [Life of John Crawford-Lindsay, seventeenth Earl of Crawford, by T. F. Henderson.] —*Stephen (L.) and Lee (S.) Dictionary of National Biography. vol.* 33. 1893.

Lindsay (John, *nineteenth Earl of Crawford and third Earl of Lindsay,* 1702-1749.) Information for the Earl of Sutherland in a suit for Precedency against the Earl of Crawford. 4to. Edinb. 1706.

— [Another edition, with additions.] sm. 4to. Edinb. 1706.—*Scottish Pamphlets, vol.* 1.

Lindsay (John, *nineteenth Earl of Crawford, etc.*)—
continued.

> The additions consist: i. At Edinburgh, the 27th
> day of September, 1705. I Sir James Murray of
> Philiphaugh, one of the Senators to the College of
> Justice, Clerk to Her Majesty's Councils, etc., do
> hereby testify and declare, that in the Records of the
> following Parliaments of King James the Third,
> King James the Fourth, King James the Fifth,
> Queen Mary, King James the Sixth, King Charles
> the First, and King Charles the Second, and in the
> Rolls of the Members present in the said several
> Parliaments, written and contained in the said
> Records, the Earls and other Members after named,
> are set down on the several days after mentioned, in
> the following order, etc. [Folding folio sheet.]—
> ii. Additional information for the Earl of Sutherland
> against the Earl of Crawford. [24 pp. n.d.]—
> iii. Memorial for the Earl of Sutherland. [4 pp. n.d.]—
> iv. Unto the Right Hon. the Lords of Council and
> Session: the Petition of John, Earl of Sutherland.
> [16 pp. n.d.]—v. Answers for John, Earl of
> Sutherland, to the Petition given in by John, Earl
> of Crawford. [7 pp. n.d.]—vi. Duplies John, Earl of
> Sutherland, to the Earl of Crawford's Remarks.
> [8 pp. n.d.]

— Copies of the Summons, and of the printed Papers,
given in to the court of Session, in the Process of
Declarator of Precedency, at the instance of the
Earl of Sutherland against the Earl of Crawford,
&c. anno 1706; and the Cases of William, Earl of

Lindsay (John, *nineteenth Earl of Crawford, etc.*)—
continued.—

Ruglen and March, and of Sir Thomas Kennedy
of Culzean, baronet, both claiming the titles and
dignities of Earl of Cassilis and Lord Kennedy,
27th January, 1762. To which is prefixed, a table
of the Pedigree of Gordon, Earl of Sutherland.
sm. 4to. Edinb. 1766.

> Containing the bookplate of the Right Hon. the Earl
> of Fife.

Lindsay (John, *twentieth Earl of Crawford and fourth
Earl of Lindsay, general,* 1702-1749.) [Life of John
Lindsay, twentieth Earl of Crawford, etc., by
T. F. Henderson.]—*Stephen* (L.) *and Lee* (S.)
Dictionary of National Biography. vol. 33. 1893.

— Memoirs of the life of the late Right Hon. John
Lindesay, Earl of Crawford and Lindesay; Lord
Lindesay of Glenesk; and Lord Lindesay of the
Byers. One of the sixteen Peers of Scotland;
Lieut.-General of His Majesty's Forces; and
Colonel of the Royal North British Grey Dragoons,
by Richard Rolt. [*Portrait, etc.*] 4to. Lond. 1753.

Lindsay (*Hon.* John, *seventh son of James, fifth Earl of
Balcarres,* 1762-1826.) Narrative of the Battle of
Conjerveram [*and*] Journal of an imprisonment in
Seringapatam.—*Lindsay* (A. W. C.) *Lives of the
Lindsays, vol.* 4. 1840.

Lindsay (*Hon.* John)—*continued.*

— [Another edition].—*Oriental Miscellanies, etc.* 1840.

Lindsay (John, *barrister-at-law and numismatist,* 1789-1870.) Notices of remarkable Greek, Roman, and Anglo-Saxon and other medieval Coins in the cabinet of the author. [3 *plates.*] 4to. Cork, 1860.

— Notices of remarkable Medieval Coins, mostly unpublished. [3 *plates.*] 4to. Cork, 1849.

— Some Observations on an ancient Talisman brought from Syria, and supposed to be the work of the Chaldæans; with engravings. 4to. Cork, 1855.

— A View of the Coinage of Ireland, from the invasion of the Danes to the reign of George IV. With some account of the ring money, etc. [14 *plates.*] 4to. Cork, 1839.

— A View of the Coinage of Scotland, with copious tables, lists, descriptions and extracts from Acts of Parliament: and an account of numerous hoards, or parcels of coin, discovered in Scotland, and of Scottish coins found in Ireland. [*Supplement, etc.; with* 23 *plates.*] 4to. Cork, 1845.

Lindsay (John, *barrister-at-law, etc.*)—*continued.*

— A View of the Coinage of the Heptarchy; to which is added a list of unpublished Mints and Moneyers of the chief or sole monarchs, from Egbert to Harold II. Also copious tables, lists, and descriptions; with an account of some of the principal hoards or parcels of Anglo-Saxon coins which have been discovered. [6 *plates.*] 4to. Cork, 1842.

— A View of the History and Coinage of the Parthians, with descriptive catalogues and tables, etc. [12 *plates.*] 4to. Cork, 1852.

Lindsay (John, *nonjuror,* 1686-1768.) [Life of John Lindsay, by W. A. Shaw.]—*Stephen (L.) and Lee (S.) Dictionary of National Biography, vol.* 33. 1893.

Lindsay (*Sir* John, *rear-admiral,* 1737-1788.) [Life of Admiral Sir John Lindsay, by J. K. Laughton.]— *Stephen (L.) and Lee (S.) Dictionary of National Biography. vol.* 33. 1893.

Lindsay (Ludovic, *sixteenth Earl of Crawford,* 1600-1652 ?) A true Relation of a Plot to betray the Towne of Poole, in the County of Dorset. And likewise how many of the Conspirators themselves were entrapped and cut off. And more particularly of the narrow escape of the Lord Craford. sm. 4to. Lond. 1643.

Lindsay (Ludovic, *sixteenth Earl of Crawford, etc.*)—*continued*.

— [Life of Ludovic Lindsay, sixteenth Earl of Crawford, by T. F. Henderson.]—*Stephen (L.) and Lee (S.) Dictionary of National Biography. vol.* 33. 1893.

Lindsay (Margaret, *Countess of Crawford and Balcarres*.) The Earldom of Mar, etc., by A. W. Lindsay, twenty-fifth Earl of Crawford, etc. [*Edited by Lady M. Lindsay.*] 1882.—*Lindsay (A.W.C.)*

— Sketches of the History of Christian Art, etc., by A. W. Lindsay, twenty-fifth Earl of Crawford, etc. [*With a " Notice," by Lady M. Lindsay.*] 1885. —*Lindsay (A.W.C.)*

Lindsay, afterwards Fordyce, afterwards Burges (*Lady* Margaret, *second daughter of James, fifth Earl of Balcarres; b.* 1753.) Versions from the German. [*In verse.*] 8vo. Wigan, 1840.—*Lindsay, afterwards Barnard (Lady Anne).*

Lindsay, afterwards Majendie (*Lady* Margaret Elizabeth) Dita. [*A novel.*] 8vo. Edinb. 1877.

Lindsay (Margaret Isabella) The Lindsays of America. A genealogical narrative and family record. Beginning with the family of the earliest settler in the mother state, Virginia, and including in an appendix all the Lindsays of America. 4to. Albany, N.Y. 1899.

Lindsay (*Miss* Maud J.) A Whitsuntide Offering [*in verse*], in aid of the Wigan Infirmary. 16mo. [Lond.] 1873.

Lindsay (Mayne) The Valley of Sapphires; illustrated by G. Montbard and others. 8vo. Lond. [1899.]

Lindsay (Patrick, *sixth Lord Lindsay of the Byres: d.* 1589.) [Life of Patrick, sixth Lord Lindsay of the Byres, by T. F. Henderson.]—*Stephen (L.) and Lee (S.) Dictionary of National Biography. vol.* 33. 1893.

Lindsay (Patrick, *archbishop of Glasgow,* 1566-1644.) [Life of Patrick Lindsay, Archbishop of Glasgow, by W. A. Shaw.]—*Stephen (L.) and Lee (S.) Dictionary of National Biography. vol.* 33. 1893.

Lindsay (Patrick, *lord provost of Edinburgh; d.* 1753.) The Interest of Scotland considered with regard to its Police in employing the Poor, its Agriculture, its Trade, its Manufactures, and Fisheries, etc. sm. 8vo. Edinb. 1733.

— Reasons for encouraging the Linnen Manufacture of Scotland, and other parts of Great Britain, humbly submitted to Parliament, etc. sm. 8vo. Lond. 1735.

Lindsay (Patrick, *lord provost of Edinburgh*)—*continued.*

— [Life of Patrick Lindsay, Provost of Edinburgh, by T. F. Henderson.]—*Stephen (L.) and Lee (S.) Dictionary of National Biography. vol.* 33. 1893.

Lindsay (*Hon.* Robert, *second son of James, fifth Earl of Balcarres*, 1754-1836.) Anecdotes of an Indian Life.—*Lindsay (A.W.C.) Lives of the Lindsays, etc. vol.* 4. 1840.

— [Another edition.]—*Oriental Miscellanies, etc.* 1840.

Lindsay (Robert, *of Pitscottie, Scottish historian*, 1500?-1565?.) The History of Scotland; from 1436 to 1565, etc. To which is added a Continuation, by another hand, till August, 1604. 2nd edition. 12mo. Glasgow, 1749.

— [The same.] 3rd edition. 12mo. Edinb. 1778.

— [Life of Robert Lindsay, of Pitscottie, by Æ Mackay.]—*Stephen (L.) and Lee (S.) Dictionary of National Biography. vol.* 33. 1893.

Lindsay, afterwards Campbell (*Lady* Sophia) Lady Sophia Lindsay.—*Fittis (R.S.) Heroines of Scotland.* 1889.

Lindsay (Thomas, *archbishop of Armagh*, 1656-1724.) [Life of Thomas Lindsay, Archbishop of Armagh, by William Reynell.]—*Stephen (L.) and Lee (S.) Dictionary of National Biography. vol.* 33. 1893.

Lindsay (Thomas M., M.A., D.D., *of Glasgow.*) The Reformation. *Dods' Handbook for Bible Classes.* 8vo. Edinb. 1882.

Lindsay (Wallace Martin, *fellow of Jesus College, Oxford.*) An introduction to Latin textual emendation, based on the text of Plautus. sm. 8vo. Lond. 1896.

Lindsay (*Sir* Walter, *of Balgavie, Catholic intriguer; d.* 1605.) Account of the present state of the Catholic Religion in the realm of Scotland in the year of our Lord 1594.—*Forbes-Leith (W.) Narratives of Scottish Catholics, etc.,* 1885.

— [Life of Sir Walter Lindsay, of Balgavie, by T. F. Henderson.]—*Stephen (L.) and Lee (S.) Dictionary of National Biography. vol.* 33. 1893.

Lindsay (William, *eighteenth Earl of Crawford, and second Earl of Lindsay,* 1644-1698.) The Speech of William, Earl of Crawford, President to the Parliament of Scotland, the twenty-second day of April, 1690. fol. Edinb. 1690.

— Correspondence of William, eighteenth Earl of Crawford, President of the Parliament and Privy Council of Scotland, and one of the Lords of the Treasury in Scotland, preserved in the Annandale Charter Chest.—*Historical Manuscripts Commission (vol.* 70.)—*Johnstone (J. J. Hope).*

Lindsay (William, *eighteenth Earl of Crawford, etc.*)—
continued.

— [Life of William Lindsay, eighteenth Earl of
Crawford, by T. F. Henderson.]—*Stephen* (*L.*)
and Lee (*S.*) *Dictionary of National Biography.*
vol. 33. 1893.

Lindsay (William, D.D., *united presbyterian minister*,
1802-1866.) Inquiry into the Christian Law, as to
the relationships, which bar marriage. 2nd edition.
sm. 8vo. London. 1871.

Lindsay (William Alexander, Q.C., *Windsor herald.*)
Pedigree of the House of Stewart. N.B.—This
pedigree, founded upon the accounts printed in
Wood's edition of Douglas' Peerage and other
printed books (with some corrections and additions),
was compiled for the Stewart Exhibition. 4to.
Lond. [1889.]

Folding sheet mounted upon Linen.

— Pedigree of the Royal House of Guelph, Dukes of
Brunswick, Kings of Great Britain and Ireland,
and of Hanover, proceeding from the House of
D'Este. Founded principally on "L'Art de
Vérifier les Dates," with a few modern notes.
4to. Lond. 1891.

Folding sheet mounted upon linen.

Lindsay (William Alexander, Q.C.)—*continued*.

— The Royal Household [1837-1897.] Dedicated to
Her Majesty. 4to. Lond. 1898.
    " This edition is strictly limited to 750 copies."

Lindsay (William Lauder, *botanist*, 1829-1880.)
Contributions to the Lichen-flora of Northern
Europe. 8vo. Lond. n.d.

— Mind in the Lower Animals in health and disease.
2 vols. 8vo. Lond. 1879.

— A Popular History of British Lichens, comprising
an account of their structure, reproduction, uses,
distribution, and classification. [*Coloured plates.*]
sm. 8vo. London. 1856.

— [Life of William Lauder Lindsay, by Thomas
Seccombe.]—*Stephen (L.) and Lee (S.) Dictionary
of National Biography. vol.* 33. 1893.

Lindsay (William Schaw, *merchant and shipowner*,
1816-1877.) History of Merchant Shipping and
Ancient Commerce, etc. With illustrations. 4 vols.
8vo. Lond. 1874-76.

— [Life of William Schaw Lindsay, by Gordon
Goodwin.]—*Stephen (L.) and Lee (S.) Dictionary of
National Biography. vol.* 33. 1893.

Lindsay, Lord Lindsay, a poem, by Ernest Jones. 8vo. n.p. n.d.

Lindsays (*Barons Spynie*) Barony of Spynie.—*Maidment (J.) Reports of Claims preferred to the Houses of Lords, etc.* 1882.

Printed by Strowger and Son, at Clarence Works, Wigan, in the County of Lancaster, and finished on the 11th day of November, 1899.

www.ingramcontent.com/pod-product-compliance
Lightning Source LLC
Chambersburg PA
CBHW022201020726
47496CB00008B/2816